WOLF-PACK ATTACK

D0356159

Adapted by Trey King

SCHOLASTIC INC.

ISBN 978-0-545-62789-4

LEGO, the LEGO logo, the Brick and Knob configurations, the Minifigure and LEGENDS OF CHIMA are trademarks of the LEGO Group. ©2014 The LEGO Group. Produced by Scholastic Inc. under license from the LEGO Group.
Published by Scholastic Inc. SCHOLASTIC and associated logos are trademarks and/or registered trademarks of Scholastic Inc.

12 11 10 9 8 7 6 5 4 3   14 15 16 17 18 19/0

Printed in the U.S.A.   40
First printing, February 2014

MIX
Paper from
responsible sources
FSC™ C020056

The Wolves go to the Croc Swamp.

The Eagles stole our Mother Tooth. We must attack!

What's the big deal about a *tooth*?

It's so much more than that, Cragger. Every member of our tribe is descended from the Great Mother Wolf.

All we have left of her is a single fang. This is the **Mother Tooth**, our most sacred relic.

The next day, Eris and Laval fly to the Wolf Camp.

Hello? Anybody home?

We heard some howls last night. Just want to make sure everyone's okay.

Eris notices a strange sign.

Uh-oh. Looks like trouble.

Meanwhile, the Crocs and Wolves prepare to attack Eagle Spire.

All right, Worriz. Use the Bellow Plant balloons to float up to the top.

Right. And we'll attach chains to the Spire so your tanks can shake it.

As the Wolves begin their attack, they don't know the Crocs have an even bigger plan in store. . . .

Heh-heh-heh.

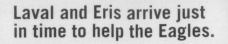

Laval and Eris arrive just in time to help the Eagles.

Eglor, you guys hold back the Wolves. I'll call for reinforcements!

CLASH!

Aim for their balloons! We'll drop them into the river!
POP!
POP!
Arooo!
SPLOOSH!
Aw, man! I hate wet fur.

Down below, Wilhurt comes up with a plan.

Everyone, let's use our ropes and hooks to climb to the Mother Tooth!

BONK!

Suddenly, he is hit by something!

Ow! What hit me?

Hee-hee. I just *love* a good book, don't you?

On the other side of the Spire, Laval calls for help.

The Lions hear his roar.

The Wolves are attacking the Eagles. And Laval is with them! We must hurry!

The Lions are on their way. We'll need jets to fly them up here.

Suddenly, the Wolves blow up the Eagles' planes!

BOOM!

Eris, your plane is the only one left. But I think I know another tribe who can help us.

Laval and Eris fly to the Raven Camp . . .

You want *us* to fly *your* army on *our* planes? Why would we do that, my friend?

Because we'll pay you.

My fellow Ravens, it looks like we're taking a trip . . . to Profit City!

Far below, the Crocs begin to pull the chains . . .

. . . and the Spire shakes!

RUMMMMBLE!

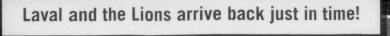

We have to cut these chains before—

Not this time, Lion!

CLASH!

WHOAAA!

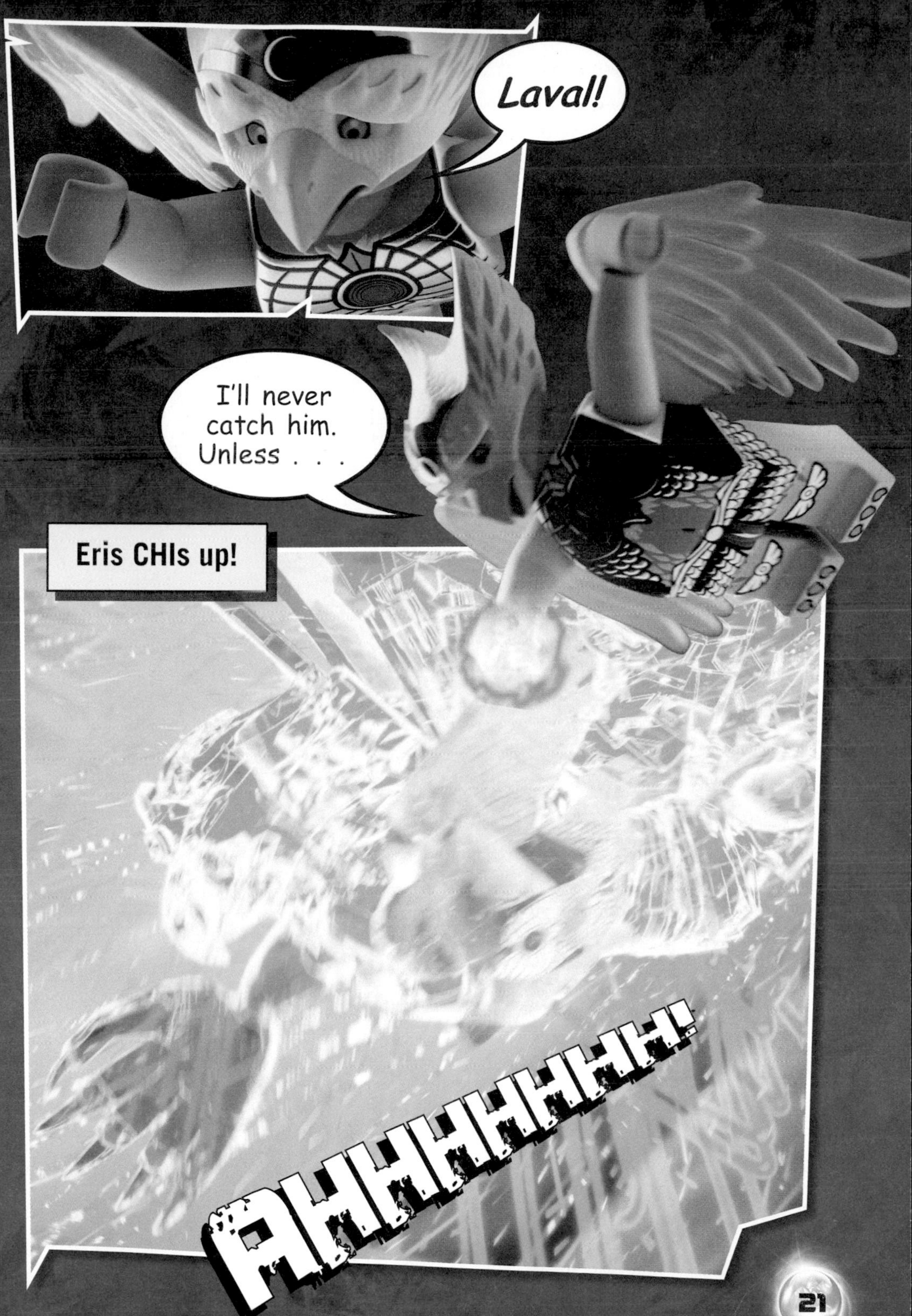

Laval!
I'll never catch him. Unless . . .
Eris CHIs up!
AHHHHHHHH!

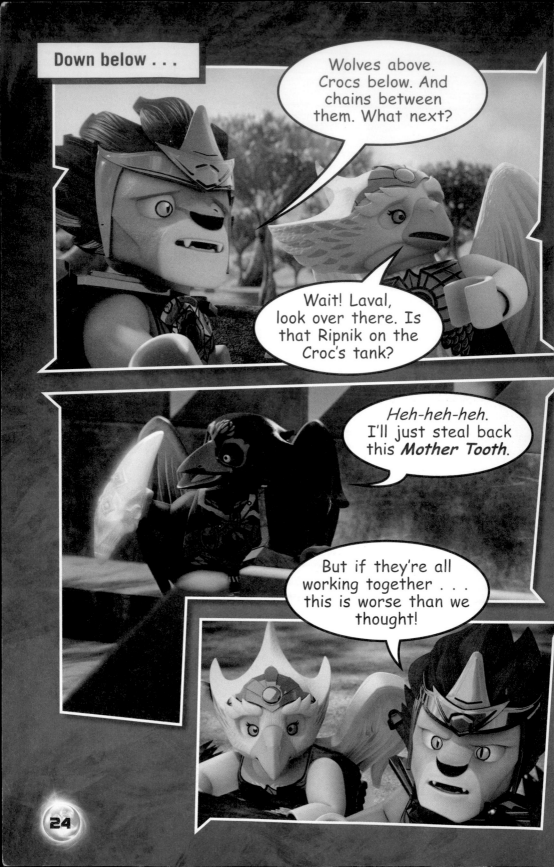

RUMBLE!

What's Cragger doing down there? He's only supposed to shake the birds out of their tower!

You should've known better than to trust Cragger. Now he can finish us all off!

CREAK!

But just when all seems lost . . .

The Ravens swoop in and blast the chains! They don't want the Crocs to destroy their best customers!

Not for Chima.
For customers!

Up above, the Wolves still want to battle.

There will be **no** peace until we get our Mother Tooth back!

Suddenly, the Mother Tooth falls from above.

THUNK!

HOWWL!

The Mother Tooth! Battle's over, everyone.

That's it?

THE END